This book belongs to:

D1275118

Printed in the U.S.A.

ISBN 0-7172-8284-8

Jim Henson's
Muppet Babies
Bean's
Boo-Boo

by Ellen Weiss   illustrated by David Prebenna

GROLIER

One day, Baby Bean was running after a
ball and fell down.

Ouch! His knee hurt! There was a scrape on it.

Bean didn't like his boo-boo. He wanted to make it go away.

Bean found Kermit on the window seat. "Kermit," he said, "I have a boo-boo. How can I make it go away?"

"I think you're supposed to wash it off," said Kermit.

"Okay," said Bean. "I'll wash it."

So Bean washed off his boo-boo with soap and water.

But when he was done, the boo-boo wasn't gone.

Bean found Fozzie next.

"Fozzie," he said, "how can I make my boo-boo go away?"

"Try putting something cold on it," said Fozzie.

So Bean put an ice cube on his boo-boo. It felt a little better. It felt a lot colder. But it didn't go away.

Along came Animal.

"Boo-boo?" he asked, looking at Bean's knee.

"Boo-boo," said Bean. "I want to make it go away."

"Animal yell at boo-boo," said Animal. "Make it go away."

Animal took a deep breath. *"Go 'way, boo-boo!"* he yelled.

"There," said Animal. "All gone?"
"It feels a little better," said Bean. "But it's still not gone."

Bean went to look for Piggy.

"Piggy," he said, "I have a boo-boo."

"Would you like me to kiss it?" asked Piggy. "I always kiss my babies when they get boo-boos."

"Yes, thank you," said Bean.

So Piggy put a nice Piggy-kiss right next to Bean's boo-boo.

It felt much, much better after that. But it didn't go away.

When Nanny saw Piggy kissing Bean's knee, she came over to see what was going on.

"Bean has a boo-boo," said Piggy.

"Would you like an extra-special bandage with stars and rainbows?" Nanny asked Bean.

"Yes, please," said Bean.

So Nanny put one of her extra-special
bandages on Bean's boo-boo.

It still didn't go away, but at least he
couldn't see it anymore.

The next couple of days were sunny, and Nanny took everyone to the playground. Bean played so much that he forgot all about his boo-boo.

A few days later, Bean's bandage fell off in the bathtub. And guess what?

Bean's boo-boo was all gone!
It had healed all by itself.

It was certainly fine to wash it and put ice on it and yell at it and kiss it and put a bandage on it.

But what Bean's boo-boo had really needed all along...

...was a little time to get better.